A Visit from the Leopard

Memories of a Ugandan Childhood

CATHERINE MUDIBO-PIWANG
and EDWARD FRASCINO

A Visit from the Leopard

Memories of a Ugandan Childhood

illustrations by James Roberts

 **Pippin Press**
New York

Pippin Press, 229 East 85th Street
Gracie Station, Box 1347
New York, NY 10028

Printed in China

10 9 8 7 6 5 4 3 2 1

Library of Congress Cataloging-in-Publication Data

Piwang, Catherine Mudibo.
    A visit from the leopard : memories of a Ugandan childhood / by
Catherine Mudibo-Piwang and Edward Frascino ; illustrations by
James Roberts.
        p.   cm.
    SUMMARY: Tells the story of Mbiro, who was named for the swiftly
racing leopard, and her childhood experiences in the Ugandan village of
Butangasi.
    ISBN 0-945912-27-7
    [1. Uganda Fiction.]   I. Mudibo-Piwang, Catherine and Frascino,
Edward.   II. Roberts, James Barlow, 1969- ill.   III. Title.
    PZ7.P68945 Vi 2000
    [Fic]—dc21
                                                    99-26992
                                                         CIP

For my grandmother, my parents and my children—and for my clan family, the Abatabonas, for giving me a belonging, a heritage.

CMP

Contents

Early Days

Bathed in the light of a full African moon shining through the window, Mbiro was born. Baba, the baby's father, waited outside in the moonlight until he heard the newborn cry.

"Is it a boy or a girl?" Baba asked, poking his head through the window.

"Come and see our fine new daughter, my husband," said his wife, Niambi.

Grandmama wrapped the baby in a soft cloth, and carefully handed the infant to her son. Baba grinned from ear to ear. He lay his daughter down beside Niambi, and took his wife's hand.

"What shall we name her?" Niambi the mother asked.

"Look!" the grandmother said. "That cloud looks exactly like a leopard racing across the moon."

"My little girl will be as swift as a leopard," Baba said. "So we will name her Mbiro."

"My son chooses well," his mother said, gazing at her new granddaughter. "Mbiro means 'one who races.'"

"Mbiro is a good name," Niambi said, kissing the head of her baby girl.

Baba and Niambi's other children huddled impatiently in the doorway.

"May we see the baby?" asked Egesa, their oldest son.

"Did you all wash your hands and faces as I told you?" their grandmother asked.

"Yes, Grandmama," they all said.

"Then you may come in one at a time to welcome your new sister," said Grandmama. "Her name is Mbiro."

1 Morning

Years had passed. Mbiro, now eight years old, turned in her bed and squinted at the ray of light streaking through the grass roof. She sighed and turned over, pulling the blanket up to her chin, for the nights and early mornings were chilly. She liked lying quietly on her soft papyrus bed, listening to the birds, and gazing up at the grass roof that interlocked like a spider's web.

The walls of Mbiro's house, a one-room hut, were round and made of red mud. The grass roof came to a point in the center. The windows, without windowpanes, were covered by shutters. Her house and the houses of her grandparents, and aunts and uncles were built in a circle around a small clearing. This group of houses was their homestead. Their clan, the Tabona Clan, was made up of ten homesteads surrounding a much larger clearing known as the Village Square. The clan traced its ancestry to one man named Were. They were known as "children of Were." The village of Butangasi where they lived is in eastern Uganda.

Slowly Mbiro pushed aside her blanket, and got up. She walked to the window, opened the shutters, and looked outside.

"What a beautiful day!" she said out loud.

The first rays of sunlight made rainbow colors on the dewy wet leaves of the mango tree just behind her house.

I must hurry, thought Mbiro, *or I will be late for school.*

Quickly she wrapped herself in her *kitenge,* a long, wide striped cloth of many colors, and hurried to the kitchen. Her parents, Baba and Niambi, were already out in the fields tending their crops. Every morning, before going to school, Mbiro had to fetch water for her Grandmama who lived on the other side of their homestead. She picked up the old water pot, and, balancing it on her head, started off for the well. On the way she hummed a tune and greeted the neighbors who were early in their garden working with baskets and sickles. The harvest of millet and corn had started.

12

"*Muliyo mutye?*" she said, which means, *How is the morning?* in the language spoken by their tribe.

"*Huliyo,*" they answered, which means, *Fine.*

Using a hollow gourd called a calabash, Mbiro scooped water from the well into her water pot. When it was full she lifted the pot onto her head and started toward Grandmama's. She walked quickly for the old pot leaked water through a thin crack. Tiny droplets trickled down behind her ear, tickling her neck.

As she approached her grandmother's hut, she called out, "Grandmama, how is the morning?"

"Fine, fine, my little one," answered Grandmama. "Eee! You are all wet. Why?"

"This pot has a crack, Grandmama."

"Time we made you a new one," Grandmama said in her strong, husky voice. "Come warm your ribs with Grandmama's porridge."

Mbiro quickly emptied the water into Grandmama's sturdy pot, and sat on the mat by the fire. She held out a calabash for Grandmama to fill with millet porridge.

"Eat slowly, little one," Grandmama said. "You gobble your breakfast like a hungry hyena."

"I don't want to be late for school," Mbiro said.

She quickly finished the porridge, and hurried toward the door.

"Your lunch!" Grandmama called after her.

"Thank you," said Mbiro picking up the lunch Grandmama had prepared. It was *omuhenye*, a sweet potato and peas mash wrapped in a scorched banana leaf.

"On your way home from school, Mbiro, gather some clay from the river bank. On Saturday I will make you a fine new water pot."

"I won't forget," said Mbiro touching her damp neck. "Good day, Grandmama."

"Good day, my little one." And they hugged each other.

Mbiro almost bumped into her Uncle Ochola on her way out. He looked very angry, and rushed past her into Grandmama's house.

"Mama!" Uncle Ochola called.

"Yes, my son," Grandmama answered.

"Someone has stolen two of my finest chickens!" Uncle Ochola exclaimed.

A thief in Butangasi Village? Mbiro wondered who it could be.

2 School

Mbiro ran back to her house. She always ran fast, like a leopard, as her grandmother would say. She unwrapped her *kitenge*, and slipped into her school uniform.

"It's a good thing this uniform is such a deep brown color," she thought. "It doesn't show any stains from the mud puddle I fell into yesterday."

She preferred the orange, yellow, green, and red stripes of her *kitenge*. It was part of a special *kitenge* her mother had often worn. But when it began to show wear, her mother had cut it into smaller pieces for Mbiro and her older sisters.

Mbiro tied the belt of her uniform, and grabbed her straw bag off a peg. As she ran out to join her brothers and sisters, she remembered the promise to her grandmother. She picked up some dry banana strippings in which to wrap the clay from the river bank.

"You are late again," said her fourteen-year-old brother, Egesa.

"Too busy watching birds this morning?" asked Mukeni, who at thirteen was often annoyed with her little sister.

"Next time we will leave for school without you," said her brother Wandera. He was ten.

Mbiro knew they would wait for her because she always led the way along the path to the Butangasi School. When she was younger, Mbiro thought it was an honor to lead the way to school, but she soon learned differently. The path was overgrown with bushes covered with dew, and whoever walked first would get wet. Sometimes the dew was very cold.

Mbiro crossed the big road followed by Egesa, Wandera, and her sisters, Mukeni, Sando, twelve, and Sinya, nine. The road ran all the way from Busia, the only town in the county, to the big lake, Lake Victoria. Butangasi, the village where Mbiro and her family lived, was not near the town nor the Lake but midway between them. The journey by foot to either place took half a day. The trip was shorter by bicycle, though not many had bicycles. Mbiro had never been to Busia.

A bus came on the big road about once a week, but the fare to Busia was too expensive.

"I cannot get into those things that move like the wind," Grandmama had said of the bus.

But Mbiro wished she could ride the bus to Busia someday.

Finally, they arrived at school. The morning games session before classes began was Mbiro's favorite part of the day. With all the screaming and laughing she wished the games would never stop. Today her sisters Sando and Sinya and her classmate Akello waited for Mbiro to join them in *chadongo*, a game similar to hopscotch.

Before they began the game, Akello remarked, "There were shops full of pretty things." She was telling of the trip to Busia she had taken with her father on his bicycle. "And electric lights were hanging everywhere."

Mbiro had never seen an electric light, only a picture of one in her school book. At night the only light in her village came from oil lamps, and sometimes the moon.

"There were orange, and yellow, and green, and

red lights," Akello continued, "and magazines with beautiful pictures on their covers."

Orange, yellow, green, and red were the colors Mbiro liked so much in the stripes of her *kitenge*. She imagined that lights in those colors would seem magical.

"Did your father buy any colored lightbulbs?" she asked Akello.

"You chicken-brain!" Akello laughed. "What good are lightbulbs in a village of mud huts? We have no electricity here."

Sando and Sinya laughed, too. Mbiro felt foolish, but she wanted so much to see the colored lights.

"My father bought me something better than lightbulbs. He bought me this magazine," Akello said, and from her straw bag she took out a magazine with shiny paper and a photo of a beautiful woman in a pink dress on the cover.

"Let me see! Let me see!" Sando and Sinya said together.

Mbiro wanted to see, too, but she was embarrassed because her sisters had laughed at her about the light bulbs.

"Now don't get it dirty," Akello said. "I am going to show it in class today."

"Oooh!" said Sando. "How pretty!"

"Look at this one," said Sinya turning the page to a photo of another beautiful woman.

Mbiro stood on her toes trying to see over her sisters' shoulders, but a glimpse of a shoe with a very tall heel was all she could see in the photo.

"That's enough," said Akello tucking the magazine safely into her straw bag. "Let's play *chadongo*."

Sando and Sinya drew squares in the dirt. First they drew big squares, and then smaller and smaller ones. Akello tossed a piece of clay into a square and then hopped on one leg, picked up the piece of clay, and hopped back to the starting point. She was very careful not to step on any of the lines or in the "no step" square. If she had she would be eliminated from the game.

Next it was Mbiro's turn. She threw the piece of clay and it landed in the smallest square farthest from the starting point.

"You'll never do it, chicken-feet," said Akello, folding her arms.

Mbiro felt as if the roots of her hair were on fire. She hopped into the first square, then into the next, and the next. When she reached the smallest square she bent down to pick up the piece of clay. The leg she hopped on was getting tired, and she almost lost her balance. She scooped up the piece of clay, turned, and began hopping back to the starting point. She wobbled a little, and had to think very hard to keep from falling over.

"B'rawk! B'rawk! B'rawk!" Akello made a sound like a chicken, and flapped her arms against her sides. "Chick-chick-chicken feet."

Mbiro's eyes filled with tears, making it hard for her to see the lines. She bit her lip to keep from crying. At last she was back at the starting point.

"I did it!" Mbiro said.

"Oh, you think so," said Akello. "Then whose footprint is that on the line?"

Mbiro looked and indeed there was a footprint on one of the lines.

"It must be yours, " Mbiro said, feeling very angry.

She looked to her sisters, hoping they would agree with her. Sando and Sinya said nothing. Suddenly the screaming and laughing all around wasn't fun anymore.

Please, please, please make the bell ring! Mbiro pleaded. At last it rang and the games session was over. Mbiro grabbed her straw bag, and ran off to the parade ground.

The parade ground was bounded on three sides by the mud and grass building of the Butangasi

School. Between the two classroom buildings was another for offices. The houses at the edge of the school grounds were living quarters for the headmaster and the teachers.

Mbiro was first in line for her grade, Primary Two. She was grateful for the classmates who fell into line behind her, ahead of Akello, who never hurried anywhere. After everyone was in line, Akello strutted onto the parade ground as if they all were waiting just for her. Mbiro's brother, Egesa, in white shirt and khaki pants, was in the Primary Seven line. Wandera, in Primary Four, wore a brown shirt and shorts. Their sisters Mukeni, Sando, and Sinya, in brown dresses, were in Primary Six, Five, and Three. On Mondays the freshly washed and ironed uniforms looked neat and clean. But this was Friday, and the uniforms showed their wear, especially the white shirts of the students in Primary Seven, except for Egesa's. He washed his shirt almost every day.

The headmaster came out of the office building, greeted the students, and led them in a school prayer. Then each line marched to their classrooms for morning roll call and their morning clean-up assignments. Primary Two, Mbiro's class, was given the task of picking up old scraps of paper and orange peels and taking them to the pit where the trash was burned.

"I hate this assignment," Akello was grumbling to one of the other girls.

No one liked it, including Mbiro. She wished they had been given the task of watering the school flower garden.

Then, pretending to pick up trash near the garden, she decided to smell the orange, purple, yellow and white flowers instead.

"Look at Mbiro," Akello said loudly. "Her nose is stuck in that flower like some fat, old bumblebee."

Quickly Mbiro gathered some scraps of paper and took them to the burning pit as the bell rang for class to begin.

All the girls rushed to their classroom, each hoping to get a front seat. The reason was Mr. Wafula, the English teacher. He was young and handsome and the son of a chief. He always dressed in a crisp white shirt, and was the only teacher besides the headmaster who wore a necktie every day. Mbiro stared at him, fascinated by the sound of his voice. English was her favorite subject.

"Good morning, class," Mr. Wafula greeted them.

"Good morning, Mr. Wafula," they chorused.

"Today we are going to put some words into sentences," Mr. Wafula said. "Who remembers what a sentence is?"

Many hands flew up including Mbiro's, but Akello's hand was first.

"Yes, Akello," Mr. Wafula said.

"A sentence," said Akello, "has a subject and a predicate. It begins with a capital letter and ends with a period or a question mark."

"Very good, Akello," Mr. Wafula said. "Who knows another punctuation mark that can end a sentence?"

Everyone was thinking. Suddenly Mbiro remembered. She raised her hand.

"Yes, Mbiro," said Mr. Wafula.

"An exclamation point!" Mbiro exclaimed.

"That's correct," Mr. Wafula said. "Very good, Mbiro." And he smiled at her.

Akello raised her hand again.

"Yes, Akello," said Mr. Wafula.

"Last week I went to Busia," Akello said, "and my father bought me this."

She waved the magazine over her head. Its colorful, shiny pages sparkled in the sunlight streaming in the window.

"Bring it here," Mr. Wafula said.

Akello strutted up to the front of the class and

stood next to the teacher as she handed him the magazine.

"This will be very helpful with our lesson today," Mr. Wafula said turning the pages of the magazine. "Thank you, Akello."

Mbiro walked home from school alone. She wished that she could do something to make Mr. Wafula proud of her.

At the riverbank she gathered the clay she had promised her Grandmama. She wrapped the clay in the dry banana strippings she carried in her straw bag. It made a nice big ball perched on top of her head as she set off for home.

When she reached the village square, she heard angry voices. Kayo and Oguma, two men from different homesteads, were shouting at each other, and a small crowd had gathered.

"You stole my goat!" Oguma said, shaking his fist.

"You are crazy, old man," Kayo said.

"You envy me," Oguma said, "because I have a goat and you do not. I demand to look in your shed!"

Mbiro could see that Oguma was so angry he was trembling.

"Maybe your goat ran away," Kayo said, "so she would not have to look at your ugly face."

Some clan members laughed, but others shouted, "Show us your shed, Kayo! Prove you are innocent!"

"No," said Kayo. "On my word as a Tabona clansman, I stole no goat."

Oguma threw a stone, hitting Kayo on the arm. Kayo picked up a stick, and chased Oguma around the square. The crowd took sides. Some cheered for Oguma, others for Kayo.

Mbiro turned toward her home. She knew that the children of Were were not thieves and that this fighting could bring shame on Butangasi.

3 A Surprise Meeting

The next morning, Mbiro awoke to the sound of wood being chopped. Rubbing her eyes, she got out of bed. The house felt unusually hot. She washed her face, tied on her *kitenge*, and opened the shutters wide. It was hot outside as well. Soon the rains would come, but it was still the dry season.

This was Saturday, and the whole family had chores to do. Egesa and Wandera were cutting logs for the fire. Mukeni, Sando and Sinya were tending the crops of millet, a cereal grain; sorghum, a thick grain for animal feed; groundnuts, and corn. Grandpapa was making a granary for storing grain from the harvest. It looked as if he were weaving a huge basket from large twigs.

As Grandpapa wove the granary, Niambi sealed the holes with mud and cow dung, and let it dry. Baba made the grass roof. With the help of his

31

sons, he would later lift the roof into place on top of the granary and secure it with ropes.

Grandpapa had woven Mbiro's straw bag, and he was also an expert wood carver.

"His hands are good at whatever he tries," Grandmama liked to say.

Mbiro loved to watch her grandfather carve all kinds of stools.

"When I was a young man, little one," Grandpapa had told her, "I was even better known for wrestling." She tried to picture Grandpapa wrestling, and the image made her smile.

With her leaky water pot atop her head, and her straw basket full of clay, Mbiro ran to fetch the water for Grandmama, as she did every day.

"This clay is good," Grandmama said, unwrapping the banana strippings from the big ball. "You did well, little one."

"I collected it yesterday on my way home from school," Mbiro said.

She wanted to tell her grandmother about school and how Akello had teased her, but it could wait until later.

Grandmama was the Tabona Clan's pot-maker. Mbiro was her helper so that she might learn pot-making herself. Grandmama's fingers moved

swiftly, kneading and molding the lump of clay. Mbiro watched closely, and right before her eyes the shapeless blob of clay formed into a lovely new pot with a long neck, smooth mouth and round belly. One day she hoped that she would make pots as beautiful as Grandmama's.

With the remaining clay, Grandmama made some bowls in different sizes.

"Look at your new pot, my son's daughter, do you like it?" Grandmama asked, holding her long-necked handiwork. "Eee! Don't touch it! Just carry it carefully to the drying shed. You don't think I can make one as good as this again, do you?"

"I love it, Grandmama," Mbiro answered.

Carefully they made their way to the shed where pots were drying. Mbiro laid her new pot down gently and helped Grandmama with the bowls she was carrying.

"Let me see if the pots we made last Saturday are ready for firing," Grandmama said.

She tapped cautiously on each. A high, cracking sound meant the pot was ready for the firing pit. She chose a few, and Mbiro transported them to the pit filled with leaves, twigs and dry grass for the fire. Grandmama lighted the fire in the pit.

The pots would bake until they were reddish-brown which meant they were done.

After a few minutes, Grandmama said, "No need for us to sit and swelter. Let us cool ourselves in the shade of the big *kituba* tree beside the stream of cool water."

Many insects buzzed around their heads as they left the village and headed for the *kituba* tree. Grandmama walked slowly. Her arms and legs were as thin as twigs but her back was straight and her eyes were sharp. Carefully she seated herself in the shade of the big tree, and heaved a deep sigh. Mbiro sat by the stream and let the cool water wash over her hot, dusty feet, kicking and splashing herself all over. The cool drops felt good.

A butterfly fluttered past her nose. She tried to catch it but a breeze carried it out of reach. Her eyes followed the brightly-colored wings until they disappeared inside a thicket of small trees. She stared into the thicket waiting for the butterfly to reappear when suddenly she saw a flash of yellow. Grandmama did not move, but her sharp eyes had seen it, too.

"Little one," she said, "walk slowly back to the village. Do not run and do not utter a sound."

Mbiro did not understand why Grandmama was sending her back alone. Slowly and quietly she started toward the village, but she was curious. She stopped and hid behind a bush, watching and waiting.

Grandmama sat as still as a stone beneath the big *kituba* tree. Slowly, from the thicket of trees, a large leopard emerged. It looked like a big, yellow cat with spots that appeared to be carefully hand-painted.

The leopard sniffed the air, and trotted gracefully toward the *kituba* tree. Its paws did not even seem to touch the ground. When the leopard saw Grandmama he stopped, tilting his head to one side. Grandmama did not move. The leopard licked his paw and rubbed it against the side of his face, just like any cat washing itself.

Mbiro's eyes were wide with wonder.

A leopard! she thought. She had seen a picture of one, and had been told many times of the leopard-shaped cloud crossing the moon on the night she was born.

The leopard was more beautiful than she had imagined, and 'swift enough to race the wind.'

Mbiro was spellbound by the beauty of this magnificent beast but when the leopard opened his mouth wide, he showed long, sharp teeth.

Suddenly she was afraid for she realized that Grandmama was in danger.

Before Mbiro could think of what to do, the leopard sprinted over a dusty hill and disappeared. Grandmama sat still as before. She did not move for a long time. The only sound was the buzzing of insects. Finally, with an effort, she stood up and walked slowly toward Mbiro's hiding place.

"I was frightened!" Mbiro cried, leaping onto the path in front of her grandmother.

"Aaiii!" Grandmama stopped short, and threw her arms up to cover her face.

"Oh, it is you, little one," she laughed. "You do move like a leopard, swift and silent."

"When I saw those great teeth, Grandmama, I feared he would bite your head off."

"He was only yawning, little one. The beasts of the forest are more frightened of us than we are of them."

"Would he have hurt you?" Mbiro asked.

"Maybe, maybe not," Grandmama said, "but I have lived a long life. It would not have been a calamity. You, on the other hand, have your whole life before you. It would be a calamity if a little one were bitten or clawed by a leopard. Why did you disobey me?"

"I was curious," Mbiro mumbled looking down at the ground.

Grandmama did not smile. She had a faraway look in her eyes.

"What are you thinking?" Mbiro asked.

"Only that perhaps Uncle Ochola's chickens were not stolen," Grandmama said, walking slowly toward the village. "Come, we will eat some *omuhenye* and then decorate your pot."

Still thinking about the leopard, Mbiro hurried to the drying shed and found her clay pot dry enough to decorate.

"This pot," Grandmama said, "I will decorate with the spots of a leopard."

She dipped her fingertips into the blue-black pigment she had brewed from roots and flowers. With her five fingers close together, she pressed them all over the surface of the pot.

"See," Grandmama said when she had finished, "just like the rosettes covering a leopard's coat, the many 'eyes' of a leopard. Now, after it is fired, little one, this will be your handsome new water pot."

Mbiro would always remember her grandmother's smiling, wrinkled face this day in the firelight.

"The leopard is swift like you," Grandmama said, "my little one who races."

4 Fear

That night the Chief of the Tabona clan called a meeting. Oil lamps burned in the mud huts as everyone hurried through their evening meal.

Mbiro washed her hands and face and tied on her *kitenge*. She checked the knot to make sure it was firm. Then she joined her family in the Village Square.

Each clan member brought a log or twigs or grass to feed the big fire burning in the square. Mbiro tossed an armful of twigs into the blaze and quickly stepped back.

"Fellow children of Were," the Chief's voice boomed. "I have gathered you here tonight to speak of a dangerous and important matter."

The oldest members of the clan, called the Wise Ones, nodded in agreement. Their long shadows loomed and wavered in the firelight. Mbiro sat on a mat between Sando and Sinya and all three held hands.

"Listen carefully to the tale our clan mate Ogule tells," the Chief said solemnly.

Mbiro shivered, and held her sisters' hands tighter.

Ogule stepped forward, limping. He was a tall, thin man who leaned on his spear for support.

"I was inspecting my rabbit traps near the edge of the forest," Ogule said in a voice as thin as he was. "I have to set traps farther and farther away, near the forest, because Munadi keeps encroaching on my traps and…"

"Ogule!" the Chief interrupted. "Still complaining? That dispute was settled long ago. Now continue."

"All of the traps were empty," Ogule went on, unhappily. "So tonight my wife will have no meat in her pot. Bad luck had become my visitor, and, as I turned to leave, I found myself staring into the eyes of a leopard."

"Ayeee!" Mukeni blurted out.

"Quiet, child," said Grandmama, who was sitting close by.

"Leopards are crafty and silent," Ogule said. "I never suspected one was so close. I felt weak and tried to scream but no words came out."

44

"The breath of a leopard will paralyze your vocal cords," a woman in the crowd whispered.

"The leopard leaped," Ogule said. "Aaiii! I thought, 'This day I am going to join my grandfathers in the beyond.' But my dogs attacked it. I felt teeth digging into my leg and I fainted."

A small child of the clan began to cry. Her mother soothed her saying, "Hush, hush. Leopards will not get you, my child."

"The next thing I remember," Ogule was saying, "my dogs were standing beside me as I lay on the ground with a bleeding leg."

A loud murmur rose from the clan as they discussed this alarming news.

"Only the Wise Ones can remember the last leopard sighting," said the Chief, and the Wise Ones nodded silently. "There has not been an outbreak of thievery in Butangasi. The leopard has eaten your chickens, Ochola, and your goat, Oguma. Guard your livestock or keep them in your houses with you."

Akello strutted over to where Mbiro stood with her brothers and sisters.

"Maybe the leopard should eat you," she said to Mbiro. "Then it would have enough meat for a while."

"Akello, don't you know that leopards don't eat

people?" Egesa said, coming to his sister's rescue. "If they are frightened they may attack and hurt you, but they will not kill you."

"Now who is a chicken-brain, Akello?" Mbiro said, feeling good.

After the meeting Mbiro was confused. The leopard she and Grandmama had seen did not harm them, but Ogule had been badly hurt. She kept thinking of those long, sharp teeth.

That night she felt afraid, even in the one-room hut with her father, mother, two brothers, and three sisters.

"I won't sleep on the mat facing the doorway," Mbiro said. "The leopard would get me first."

"Then sleep in the farthest corner," Mukeni suggested.

"No, no," Mbiro said. "I don't want to be the last."

"Then sleep in the middle between Mukeni and me," said Sinya.

"Yes," agreed Mbiro, "that is best."

"Sleep well, children of mine," Niambi said, blowing out the oil lamp. "Leopards may indeed be clever but they cannot open doors or squeeze through windows."

"Sleep well, Mother," all the children answered.

47

The next day was Sunday. Grandmama was busy in the bushes gathering plants and leaves. Mbiro approached and asked if she could help.

"No, no, Mbiro," Grandmama said, "you cannot help me with this. It is serious and important. You must not even see what I am doing."

So everyone kept away from Grandmama as she gathered, roasted, pounded, and boiled. This was something Mbiro had never known to happen. She had always helped Grandmama dig roots and collect leaves to make medicines for coughs, malaria, and stomachaches. She wondered why she couldn't even talk to Grandmama today. In fact Grandmama could not greet or talk to anyone or eat food with anyone all day.

After the evening meal Baba gathered all his children around and explained what they must do.

"All day," Baba said, "Grandmama has been preparing a special potion to protect us from leopard attacks. You will go to Grandmama's house one by one. Egesa, the oldest, first. Mbiro, the youngest, last. You must walk backward so your shadow does not remain behind. Do not speak a word from the door of our house all the way to Grandmama's. Drink the potion and walk backward all the way home. Then go to bed and no talking until morning."

48

Fear

When Mbiro, walking backward, reached her grandmother's house, she stood silently. Grandmama appeared from behind, her face painted. She rattled a gourd filled with seeds. Dipping a calabash into a pot she drew out the potion and Mbiro drank it. It was sour. Grandmama rubbed some leaves across Mbiro's neck, chest, and face, and disappeared.

Mbiro walked home backward, and went to bed without a word to anyone. She had never seen her grandmother as she was that night, very serious and mysterious. The next morning, however, Grandmama was her usual cheerful self. She warned them that they were not to talk of taking the potion. Not to anyone.

Before going to school Mbiro asked her mother, "Mama, will the leopard go back into the forest?"

"Perhaps," her mother said, "but today the hunters and their dogs will begin hunting him."

"Will they have to kill him?" Mbiro asked.

"Yes," her mother said.

Mbiro feared the leopard but wished there was some other way to be rid of him.

"Our life is not easy, little one," her mother said. "If the leopard eats our chickens, cows and goats there will be no eggs, cheese or milk, and the village will go hungry."

"Can't the hunters just chase the leopard away?" Mbiro said, remembering the beautiful animal she had seen.

"Life is hard for the beasts of the forest, too," her mother explained. "It is not easy for them to find food. The leopard would not go away until it had eaten all our livestock."

"I hope the hunters don't find him," Mbiro said. "Maybe he'll find enough to eat in the forest and won't come back."

"Perhaps," her mother said. "Now off to school with you." And she kissed her daughter on the forehead.

5 The Leopard

That morning the students at Butangasi School lined up in the parade ground just as they did every morning. Since it was Monday, the school uniforms were all freshly washed and ironed.

Today Mr. Wafula was giving his class a spelling test.

"The first word is *ghost*," the teacher said. "*Ghost*," he repeated.

Mbiro wrote "*g*" on her paper but couldn't remember if the next letter was "*h*" or "*o*". She quickly wrote *g-h-o-s-t* on her test paper, and hoped it was correct.

"The next word is *rain*," Mr. Wafula said. "*Rain*."

All heads were bent over desks as the children wrote when, without warning, they heard the BOOM! BOOM! BOOM! of the village drums.

Everyone looked up in confusion. They understood that the tone of the drums meant danger. The BOOMs became louder and faster.

"Remain seated, everyone," Mr. Wafula said. "I will find out what is happening," and he hurried from the room.

The children began talking all at once trying to guess what was going on. Akello acted as if she knew.

"Just another family feud," she said with a smirk.

Through the open window Mbiro saw Mwaga, the school porter, rapidly peddling his bicycle toward the headmaster's office. The bicycle crashed to the ground as Mwaga jumped off and shouted, *"Engwe! Engwe yiri mu Butangasi!"* ("A leopard! A leopard in Butangasi village!")

In the classroom all eyes were wide with fear.

"I want to go home!" Akello said, rushing toward the open window.

"No!" Mbiro cried, blocking her way.

"We'll be trapped in here if the leopard comes," Akello said, and she tried to push past Mbiro.

"Leopards don't kill people," Mbiro said, gripping Akello's arm.

"They can hurt you bad," Akello said, "and scar

you for life. Ogule will carry the leopard's mark on his leg forever."

Mbiro closed the shutters, darkening the classroom.

"I want my mother," Akello said with a sob in her throat. "I'm afraid."

Faced with real danger, she was not so confident and sassy.

Is this the same girl who can bully me to tears? Mbiro thought.

"Leopards cannot open doors and windows," Mbiro said, echoing her mother. "We are safe inside."

Suddenly Mr. Wafula came running back into the classroom.

"Everyone sit down." he said. "It's so dark in here. Who closed the shutters?"

"I did," Mbiro said.

"Yes, of course," Mr. Wafula said. "I should have thought of it myself. You acted intelligently, Mbiro," and he patted her on the shoulder. Mbiro glowed inside. At last she had made Mr. Wafula proud of her.

The drums stopped. Now Mbiro heard dogs barking and the hunter's bells. They were hunting the leopard. She worried about her family and hoped they were safe behind locked doors and windows.

"Hold my hand," Akello said as she sat beside Mbiro.

The whole class sat silently in the dark, listening. Only their ears could tell them what direction the hunt was taking. In the silence, Mbiro thought everyone could hear her heart pounding.

The barking dogs and hunter's bells grew louder. They were nearing the school!

One of the boys opened the shutters slightly and peeked outside. Mr. Wafula did not stop him. Slowly Mbiro and the others moved toward the opening window, all except Akello, who crouched under a desk. She trembled so hard her teeth chattered. As the shutters opened wider, the noise of the dogs and hunters was deafening.

Mbiro saw a cloud of dust.

"The leopard!" she cried.

They all saw it. The leopard came out of the dust and sprinted across the parade ground. The animal's movements were magical. It seemed to be running on air. Mbiro wished she could watch it forever, but it quickly disappeared across the courtyard.

Almost immediately barking dogs and shouting hunters ran across the courtyard in pursuit.

She remembered her grandmother saying, "The beasts of the forest are more frightened of us than we are of them."

Poor leopard, Mbiro thought, *alone against all those dogs and men.*

She began to grow angry at the hunters, and prayed the leopard would make it safely back into the forest.

The other children became excited by the chase. They made bets on who among the hunters would make the kill. Mbiro hated the pleasure they took in the hunting of that beautiful animal. All of a sudden there was an uproar of voices and barking louder than any she had heard before.

"The leopard is dead!" Mwaga shouted as he circled the parade ground.

Cheers of victory rose up throughout the school. Mbiro's classmates joined in the shouting. No one noticed Mbiro's tears.

The children scrambled out of the classroom, some through the door, some through the window. They looked happy. Now that the danger had past, Akello was her usual self again.

"Come on, you ant!" she called to Mbiro. "Don't you want to see?"

Mbiro looked away.

Mr. Wafula sat quietly at his desk. He looked as if he were about to say something, but Mbiro did not wait. She grabbed her straw bag and ran out of the classroom.

She ran away from the shouts and cheers. She wanted to remember the leopard gliding gracefully through the air, not lying lifeless in the dirt. She ran faster. Her feet never seemed to touch the ground. Tears streaked her cheeks. She ran to Grandmama.

"Grandmama! Grandmama!" Mbiro called as she ran across the compound.

Grandmama's house was empty. All of the houses were empty. From the Village Square came sounds of stomping feet and clanging bells as the hunters began their victory dance. The chief's horn blew, and the village soloist sang the victory song accompanied by the *nanga*, a stringed instrument. Everyone was there, but Mbiro could not believe her grandmother would be celebrating the death of the leopard.

She sat outside her grandmother's house, and covered her ears with her hands. She didn't want to hear the victory celebration. Men and women passed by carrying baskets of smoked fish, goat meat and chickens, beans, millet, and cassava flour. Some carried firewood and pots of millet beer. They all swayed to the beat of the ceremonial drums. The victory feast would last long into the night.

"Come to the feast," people shouted to Mbiro, but she turned her back on them.

Finally she saw her grandmother walking slowly toward her. Grandmama did not sway to the drumbeat, and her face was solemn.

"Grandmama!" Mbiro called, running to meet her.

The old woman rested her hand on her grand-daughter's shoulder.

"Why did the hunters kill it?" Mbiro said, and she began to cry.

Grandmama put her arms around her.

"They had to make the village safe, little one," she said.

"Why didn't they just chase the leopard away?" Mbiro sobbed.

"It would have returned when it was hungry," Grandmama said. "But the spirit of the leopard did not die. Come, you will see."

The old woman led her granddaughter toward the victory celebration.

The hunters, dressed in colorful feathers with bells on their ankles, were dancing in a circle. On a mat, in the center of the circle lay the dead leopard. One by one the hunters broke from the circle, and knelt beside the dead beast. Each one spoke to the animal, and embraced it.

"They honor the leopard's spirit," Grandmama said, "and explain the reason it had to be killed. They beg the spirit to forgive them, and ask that their act of destruction will not disturb the harmony between man and nature."

Mbiro remembered the first time she saw the leopard peacefully washing its face. It was sad to see it lying so still.

When all the hunters had honored the leopard, the chief followed with his tribute to the slain animal.

"Children of Were," spoke the chief, "honor the powerful spirit of this great beast."

One at a time members of the Tabona Clan began kneeling beside the leopard.

Grandmama took Mbiro's hand.

"Let us honor the leopard's spirit, Mbiro," she said.

Now Mbiro realized that the leopard had simply been true to its nature. When hungry, it ate. When frightened, it attacked. Sadly, the hunter's way was the only way to keep Butangasi safe.

Mbiro knelt beside the body. She saw how

perfectly the leopard's spots matched those on her water pot. She reached out and gently stroked the beautiful yellow coat.

"Forgive us," she said.